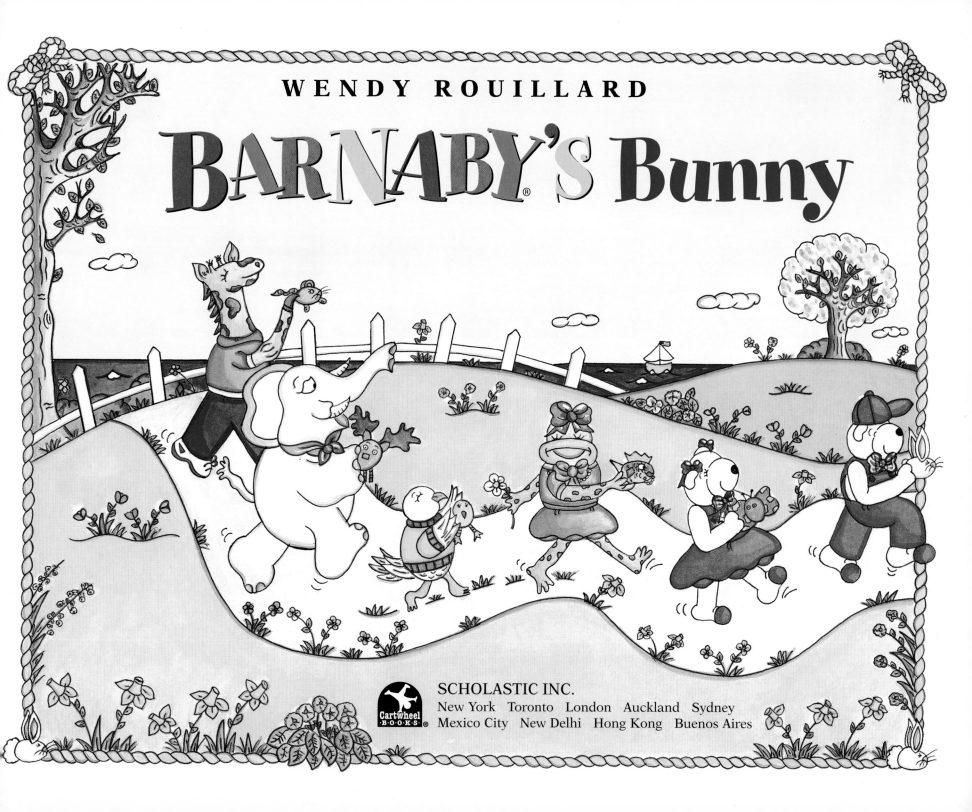

WENDY ROUILLARD

BARNABY'S Bunny

SCHOLASTIC INC.
New York Toronto London Auckland Sydney
Mexico City New Delhi Hong Kong Buenos Aires

To Parents and Educators

Character education helps children develop skills and values that enhance their awareness of themselves and others in order to solve real problems and to make good decisions. In each Barnaby book, Barnaby and his friends encounter a variety of issues familiar to young children. They learn the importance of honesty, self-discipline, empathy, respect, and other elements of character education. Developing a dialogue with children about Barnaby can help turn a reading experience into an opportunity for character education.

In *Barnaby's Bunny*, Barnaby learns the meaning of **responsibility**. He also comes to see the importance of being **honest**, even when telling the truth isn't an easy thing to do.

You can foster **honesty** and **responsibility** in the home or classroom in the following ways:

1. Hold a class or family meeting to discuss **responsible** behavior in different settings: on the playground, in a store, in a car or bus, and so on. Ask children to list behaviors for each area that would be considered **responsible** and irresponsible. Discuss possible outcomes for **responsible** and irresponsible actions.

2. Commend children for **honest** and **responsible** behavior.

3. Discuss the different **responsibilities** of children and adults in the classroom and/or at home.

4. Assign children age-appropriate jobs, but remind children that being **responsible** isn't just about doing the chore. It's following through on your commitments, not relying on others to remind you of what needs to be accomplished, and thinking things through in order to make good choices.

5. Model **honest** and **responsible** behavior for children. They are listening to what you say and watching what you do all the time.

Using the enclosed materials, children can make their own special pet eggs. Caring for a pet—even a pretend pet— is one way that children can learn the importance of **honesty** and **responsibility**, as Barnaby does in *Barnaby's Bunny*.

Janice Yelland, M.Ed.
Educational Consultant

For Daphne Bradbury,
a true best friend who has a
special fondness for bunnies.

12 11 10 9 8 7 6 5 4 3 2 1   03 04 05 06 07
Printed in China • First Scholastic printing, February 2003 • 62

On a faraway land, many miles out to sea,
There lives a young bear named Barnaby.
He is sweet and clever and cuddly, too.
He may be a bear, but he's like me and you.

Now Barnaby's friends think of something they need,
A new classroom pet to love and to feed,
But pets will require, as they will soon see,
Not only good care but responsibility.

Spring had arrived on Faraway Island. The daffodils were blooming, the ocean was sparkling, and it was show-and-tell day at school. Barnaby was bringing his dog, Baxter.

When Barnaby arrived at Academy Hill,
his classmates gathered around him.
"Hi, Baxter," said Baisley.
"Wow, what a cool dog!" said Ellery.
The bell rang and everyone rushed inside.

"It's time for show-and-tell," said Mrs. Sealey.
"Who would like to go first?"
Barnaby raised his paw.

"This is my dog, Baxter," said Barnaby.
"He's a basset hound. He can do lots of tricks."

"I wish we could have a pet in school
all the time," said Baisley.
That gave Barnaby a great idea.
"Mrs. Sealey, can we get a class pet?" he asked.
Barnaby's classmates thought it was one of the best ideas
Barnaby had ever had.
"Well, maybe..." said Mrs. Sealey. "Let me think about it."

Barnaby and his classmates were on their best behavior for the rest of show-and-tell. And for the rest of the day.

That night Mrs. Sealey thought   and thought   and thought about getting a class pet.

The next morning, Mrs. Sealey made an announcement. "Each of you will make a pet egg," she said.

"What's that?" asked Barnaby.

"It's an egg that you will decorate to look like a pet," said Mrs. Sealey. "You'll have to keep it safe, happy, and clean. If you can show me that you are responsible, then we can get a real class pet."

How To Care For
Your Pet Egg!

#1 DO NOT EAT IT

#2 GIVE IT PLENTY OF ATTENTION

#3 KEEP IT CLEAN

#4 DO NOT LET IT FALL AND BREAK

Barnaby and his classmates followed Mrs. Sealey inside to the art corner. There were cartons of hard-boiled eggs, tubes of glitter, and fur and felt in flashy colors.

Barnaby's friends were a bit nervous.
"I've never taken care of a pet before," said Baisley.
"What if I drop mine?" said Fancy Freda.
"What if I lose it?" said Jimmy.

But Barnaby was not worried.
He was a professional when it came to pet care.

He walked Baxter every day,

played with him after school,

and fed him dinner.

When Baxter was dirty,
Barnaby bathed him.

When Baxter was sick,
Barnaby gave him medicine.

Barnaby wanted to be a world-famous veterinarian when he grew up. That is, if he didn't become a world-famous explorer.
"Don't worry," Barnaby said to his friends.
"This is going to be easy."

Barnaby and his classmates worked hard all morning creating their pet eggs.

Baisley made a butterfly.

Jimmy made a gerbil.

Cece made a chick.

Ellery made an elk.

Fancy Freda made a fancy fish.

And Barnaby made a bunny.

That day on the playground, no one wanted to play.
Except for Barnaby.

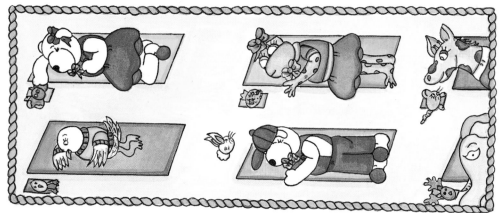

During nap time, no one could sleep.
Except for Barnaby.

And at snack time, no one was hungry.
Except for Barnaby…
well, and Ellery.

Soon it was time to go home.
"Take good care of your pet eggs," called Mrs. Sealey.
"Don't worry," said Barnaby. "This is going to be easy."

On the way home from school, Barnaby stopped to see his parents at the Main Street Market. He could smell his mother's freshly baked Cobblestone Cookies as he walked through the door.

"This is my new pet bunny," said Barnaby.
"It's nice to meet you," said Barnaby's mother.
"Now you have two pets to take care of," said Barnaby's father. "You'll have your paws full."
"Don't worry," said Barnaby. "This is going to be easy."

That afternoon everyone took extra good care of their pet eggs.

Well . . . almost everyone.

The next morning Barnaby met his friends at the school boat stop. "Ahoy there, mates! Hop on board the school boat express," shouted Hector. "Choppy waters ahead. Hold on tight to your pet eggs."

The school boat went *bumpidy-bumpidy-bumpidy, bumpidy-bumpidy-bumpidy.*

Then the school boat went *bumpidy-bumpidy splash* as it hit a huge wave. Barnaby's bunny flew out of his paws. It somersaulted and spun in the sky.

But when Barnaby arrived at school, he noticed that his
bunny had a crack down its back.
"Now we're not going to get a class pet," said Cece.
"If you hold it like this, no one will ever know," said Jimmy.
"What are you going to tell Mrs. Sealey?" asked Baisley.

"I don't know,"
said Barnaby.

"Gather around for circle time," said Mrs. Sealey.
"What did you learn about taking care of your pets?"
"You have to watch your pet very carefully," said Cece.
"You have to play with your pet very gently," said Baisley.

"Barnaby, how did you do with
your pet egg?"
asked Mrs. Sealey.

Everyone looked at Barnaby.
"Umm ... my bunny had an accident,"
he said softly.
Then he told Mrs. Sealey the whole story.

"I guess it wasn't as easy as I thought it would be," said Barnaby. "I should have been more careful." "Yes," said Mrs. Sealey. "But accidents happen. I'm glad you told me the truth."

"Is there any way to fix my bunny?" asked Barnaby. "I think there just might be," said Mrs. Sealey. She reached into her pocket and took out a tiny bandage. "Does that mean we can still get a class pet?" asked Cece. Mrs. Sealey smiled.

"Follow me," she said. "Let's give our pet eggs some exercise."
Barnaby and his classmates followed Mrs. Sealey down the hill,

and up Cobblestone Alley.

around the harbor,

"Where are we going?" asked Barnaby.
"It's a surprise," said Mrs. Sealey.

As they rounded the corner, they saw the Island Farm Stand.
Inside a wooden hutch sat a fluffy white bunny.
"Meet your new class pet!" said Mrs. Sealey.
Everyone cheered.
"Having a class pet may not be easy," said Barnaby.
"But it sure will be fun!"